A Note from

Her C

The seventh-grade camping trip was all anyone talked about at school. Everyone would sleep in tents, and I planned to share one with my best friends, Darcy and Allie. All I had to do was talk my father into it. *Finally* my dad said I could go. That was the good news. Then there was the bad news. . . . But before I tell you all about it, let me explain about my family—my very big family.

Right now there are nine people and a dog living in our house—and for all I know, someone new could move in at any time. There's me, my big sister, D.J., my little sister, Michelle, and my dad, Danny. But that's just the beginning.

Uncle Jesse came first. My dad asked him to come live with us when my mom died, to help take care of me and my sisters.

Back then, Uncle Jesse didn't know much about taking care of three little girls. He was more into rock 'n' roll. So Dad asked his old college buddy, Joey Gladstone, to help out. Joey didn't know anything about kids, either—but it sure was funny watching him learn!

Having Uncle Jesse and Joey around was like having three dads instead of one! But then something even better happened—Uncle Jesse fell in love. He married Becky Donaldson, Dad's cohost on his TV show, *Wake Up San Francisco*. Aunt Becky's so nice—she's more like a big sister than an aunt.

Next, Uncle Jesse and Aunt Becky had twin baby boys. Their names are Nicky and Alex, and they are adorable!

I love being part of a big family. Still, things can get pretty crazy when you live in such a full house!

FULL HOUSE™: Stephanie novels

Phone Call from a Flamingo
The Boy-Oh-Boy Next Door
Twin Troubles
Hip Hop Till You Drop
Here Comes the Brand-New Me
The Secret's Out
Daddy's Not-So-Little Girl

Available from MINSTREL Books

Daddy's Not-So-Little Girl

Lucinda Thomas

A Parachute Press Book

PUBLISHED BY POCKET BOOKS

New York London Toronto Sydney Tokyo Singapore

A MINSTREL PAPERBACK *Original*

A Minstrel Book published by
POCKET BOOKS, a division of Simon & Schuster Inc.
1230 Avenue of the Americas, New York, NY 10020

A Parachute Press Book

ISBN: 0-671-89860-4

First Minstrel Books printing January 1995

10 9 8 7 6 5 4 3 2 1

Cover photo by Schultz Photography

Printed in the U.S.A.

CHAPTER 1

◆ ◄ ■ ◆

"Stephanie! You're back!" Darcy said. It was Thursday morning, and Stephanie Tanner bounded down the school hallway toward her two best friends, Allie Taylor and Darcy Powell. They were standing by Darcy's locker, and Stephanie could tell from the broad smiles on their faces that they were happy to see her.

"How are you feeling?" Allie asked.

"One hundred times better," Stephanie said, slipping a strand of her long blond hair behind her ear. "You wouldn't believe how bored I was staying at home in bed for so long. It was so boring that I now know all of Michelle's stuffed animals by name.'' Stephanie shared a bedroom with her eight-year-old sister, Michelle.

''At least you got to miss a lot of super-dull classes,'' Darcy said as she closed the door of her locker.

''That part was cool at first, but after a few days I was totally miserable,'' Stephanie said. ''I was so nauseous all the time from the stomach flu that I didn't feel like doing anything. All I could eat was Jell-O and crackers. Even watching television got to be a major bore.''

''Every time I called you, your dad said you were asleep,'' Allie said. ''What a nightmare.''

''You know Dad,'' Stephanie said, rolling her eyes. ''He thought I was too weak to pick up the phone. Anyway, I tried to call you guys last night to tell you I'd be back today, but both your lines were always busy.''

''Oh, right,'' Darcy said. ''We were on a three-way call with Hilary.''

''Hilary?''

''Maybe you don't remember her,'' Allie said. ''She's new. I think you met her the first day she was here, and then the next day you got sick.''

''Hey, there she is now.'' Darcy waved to a

cute girl with curly red hair and freckles who was walking down the hall in their direction. "Allie and I spent a lot of time with her while you were home sick," she said to Stephanie. "You'll like her, Steph. She's really fun."

"Hey, guys!" Hilary said as she came up to the group. "Hi, Stephanie. I know we've just barely met, but Allie and Darcy talk about you so much, I feel like I've known you forever. I'm glad to see you're all better now."

"Thanks. It's great to be back," Stephanie said. "In fact, I've never been so happy to be in school. What did I miss? What's everybody been up to?"

Allie, Darcy, and Hilary all looked at each other and laughed. Stephanie forced a giggle, although she had no idea what the joke was.

"What's so funny?" she asked. "Did I miss something?"

"It's just that a lot happened while you were gone," Darcy explained.

"Yeah, let's just say that our lives certainly weren't boring," Allie said.

"Can somebody fill me in?" Stephanie pressed.

"Well, for one thing, the three of us went to

the mall together last weekend and we all got fake tattoos," Darcy said.

"It was so funny, Steph. You should've been there. When we went to Hilary's house to spend the night, her parents went ballistic," Allie said before she burst into hysterical laughter.

Hilary was laughing so hard that she had to hold her stomach. "My mother was practically in tears. My poor parents thought the tattoos were real."

"We explained to them right away that they were just temporary and that they'd come off in the shower, but they didn't believe us at first," Darcy said.

"So we got the idea to try to trick other people," Allie said, still laughing. "The next morning we went back to the mall and got more tattoos, then we went to Bobby Fowler's party that night and freaked everyone out."

"We totally fooled everyone," Hilary said, grinning. "We were the talk of the party."

"I didn't even know Bobby was having a party," Stephanie said.

"We thought about calling you, but we knew you were sick and wouldn't be able to go anyway," Allie said. "We were afraid it might make you feel worse if you knew about it but couldn't go."

Allie's right, Stephanie thought. *I would have felt awful. I really missed out on a lot while I was sick.* "Well, was it fun?" she asked.

"It was one of the best parties all year," Darcy blurted out. She stopped a moment and looked at Stephanie. "I'm sorry. I guess you don't want to hear how much fun the party was."

"That's okay," Stephanie said. "I'm glad you guys had a good time."

"Well, now you're back, and we're totally glad about that," Darcy said. "We really missed you."

"I missed you, too," Stephanie said. "So what else is happening?"

Allie snapped her fingers. "The seventh-grade field trip! Did you hear about it, Steph?"

"Oh, right, the overnight camp-out," Stephanie said. "My dad got a notice in the mail."

"It's going to be an absolute blast," Hilary said. "My older brother, Jim, said that on last year's trip a group of guys got together and set up a haunted house in one of the tents. They had gigantic spiders that were *real.* And gross stuff, like bags of cold macaroni that they said were real guts. Some of the girls stayed up all night scared to death because of it."

"Your brother went to this school last year?" Stephanie asked. "I thought you just moved to town."

"We always lived here; I just went to a different school," Hilary explained as she smoothed back a red curl that had fallen in her face.

"It must have been kind of hard, leaving your friends," Stephanie said.

"It was, but I'm lucky." Hilary smiled at Allie and Darcy. "I've already made some great friends here."

"Hey, maybe we'll all get to be in a tent together," Darcy said.

"Sounds great," Stephanie agreed. "I just hope my dad lets me go."

"What do you mean?" Darcy looked shocked. "Why wouldn't he let you go?"

"Because I've been sick, and he's afraid I might have a relapse," Stephanie explained with a sigh. "You know him—he's a super-worrier."

"But he has to let you go, Steph," Allie said. "I mean, you absolutely can't miss out on this!"

"I know," Stephanie said, starting to feel anxious. "But I'm going to have to do some pretty heavy persuading to get him to sign that permission slip!"

By the time Stephanie got to science, the last class of the day, she was feeling even more anxious. The camping trip was all anyone was talking about. *It's going to be the coolest trip in the history of the school,* she thought. *And Dad's not even sure he'll let me go!*

"Oh, Steph, we forgot to tell you," Allie said as Stephanie walked into the room with her and Darcy. "Darcy and I are going to the mall with Hilary after school to get some stuff for the trip. Hilary has to get a sleeping bag, and I need some sunglasses. Want to come with us?"

"Sure!" Stephanie said. She'd been feeling a little left out, hearing about the three-way phone call and all the fun Allie and Darcy had had with Hilary while she was sick. A trip to the mall with her friends was just what she needed. "I'll call home and get permission right after class."

"Okay, people. I want everyone's undivided attention," Mrs. Walker said as the students took their seats. "It's time to talk about the field trip. I'm sure you know that it's next weekend, and I'm still waiting for permission slips from some people."

Stephanie felt a little shiver. What if her father didn't sign the slip? *That's crazy,* she told herself. *Once he realizes how important the trip is, he won't let me miss it.*

"So when you go home tonight," Mrs. Walker went on, "be sure to remind your parents to get those slips back to me by Monday."

Good, Stephanie thought. *That gives me tomorrow and the whole weekend to persuade Dad.*

"Psst! Stephanie!"

Stephanie was startled from her thoughts by Mia Mantell, the girl who sat next to her. Mia had blond hair and tons of cool clothes, and she could be funny sometimes. But she could be annoying, too. She talked a lot, but she never really listened to what anyone else had to say. It was like she wanted to be the center of attention.

"Could I borrow a pen?" Mia whispered. "I forgot mine."

"Okay." Stephanie got a pen out of her book bag and handed it over. *At least I have plenty of pens,* she thought. Earlier in the year, Mia had borrowed her science notes and lost them.

Mia started drawing something, but Stephanie didn't look to see what it was. She wanted to hear what Mrs. Walker had to say.

"I know you're eager to find out who your tent partners will be," Mrs. Walker said.

"Psst! Steph!" It was Mia again.

"Wait a sec," Stephanie whispered.

Mrs. Walker stopped talking and frowned at the two girls. Stephanie tried to look innocent. Mrs. Walker absolutely hated people whispering in her class, but Mia just didn't seem to notice.

"Now, then," Mrs. Walker went on, "I haven't made the tent assignments yet, but I'll be working on that tonight, and I'll post a partial list sometime tomorrow."

"Steph!" Mia was nudging Stephanie in the side this time. "Look."

"Later, Mia, okay?" Stephanie whispered. "I want to hear this."

"Stephanie Tanner," Mrs. Walker said with another frown. "If you want to hear, then I suggest you and Mia stop talking."

Stephanie felt her face turn red.

"I *can* tell you that there will be either two or three people to a tent," Mrs. Walker went on.

Stephanie grinned at Darcy and Allie, who sat on the other side of the room. She was sure Mrs. Walker would match her up with them, since everyone knew they were best friends.

"Now, let's go on to the list of supplies that was sent home with the permission slips," Mrs. Walker said. She started reading the list.

Mia nudged Stephanie again. "You've got to see this, Stephanie," she whispered, holding out a piece of paper. Her big blue eyes were sparkling.

"Later," Stephanie whispered, trying not to move her lips.

"But it's hysterical!" Mia insisted.

To keep Mia quiet, Stephanie took the paper. On it Mia had drawn an unflattering picture of Mrs. Walker in an army outfit.

"It looks just like her, doesn't it?" Mia said with a giggle.

It did, but Stephanie didn't dare laugh. "Mia, come on," she said. "We're going to get in trouble."

"All right!" Mrs. Walker stopped reading the list of supplies and glared at Stephanie and Mia.

"Since you two can't be bothered to listen *during* class, you can stay *after* class. That way, I can make sure you hear every word."

Mia shrugged, but Stephanie was fuming. How rude! Her first chance in two weeks to go to the mall with her friends and she was stuck in detention, just because of Mia! Now Darcy and Allie and Hilary would go without her. She felt left out all over again.

Suddenly the camping trip was more important than ever. *If I don't get to go,* Stephanie thought, *my entire social life will have a total relapse!*

CHAPTER 2

"Dad?" Stephanie said at dinner that night. "Mrs. Walker wants the permission slips for the field trip in by Monday. So could you please sign it for me?"

"Well, this is only Thursday," said Stephanie's father, Danny. "There's plenty of time."

"Yeah, but as soon as I get it in I'll find out who my tentmates are," Stephanie said. "And I want to be sure I'm in the same tent as Darcy and Allie."

"I understand, honey," Danny said, helping himself to some mashed potatoes. "But I still haven't made up my mind."

"Dad!" Stephanie protested. "Look at me. I'm better. I'm totally, one hundred percent healthy!"

"You coughed in your sleep last night," Michelle said. "It woke me up."

Stephanie frowned at her little sister. "Thanks a lot, Michelle."

"I wish *I'd* been woken up," Aunt Becky said with a yawn. "Unfortunately, I don't think I ever got to sleep."

"Are the twins still keeping you up late?" asked D.J., Stephanie's big sister.

Nicky, one of the three-year-old twins, laughed happily. "Late," he said.

Alex, Nicky's brother, joined in. "Late, late, late!"

"Let's put it this way," Uncle Jesse said to D.J. "Becky and I both feel like walking zombies."

Joey, who was a comedian, couldn't resist. "You look a little like zombies too," he said with a laugh.

"Zombies," echoed Alex.

"Dad, I promise I'm not sick anymore," Stephanie said. "Besides, the trip is a whole week away. And it's super-important. I mean, it's the trip of the century. I might as well change schools if I don't go!"

"Honey, I haven't said that you definitely can't go," Danny told her. "And I know you feel fine now, but you were sick for almost two weeks. I just want to keep an eye on you for another day or so until I'm satisfied that you're well enough to go."

As Stephanie got up to clear the table, she tried to keep calm. But inside, she was fuming. *I'm sure nobody else in the seventh grade has a father who is so protective.*

After her kitchen duty was over, Stephanie tried to call Allie. She needed somebody to complain to, and Allie was always sympathetic. Besides, she wanted to find out what her friends had bought at the mall.

Allie's line was busy, so Stephanie tried Darcy. Darcy would tell her not to worry, to stay cool and everything would work out.

Darcy's line was busy, too.

Stephanie waited fifteen minutes, then tried again. Both lines were still busy. *Are they talking to each other, or is Hilary part of the conversation too?* she wondered. Before Stephanie got the flu, *she'd* always been the third member of the three-way calls.

With a sigh, Stephanie went to her room to tackle the tons of makeup work her teachers had given her. Michelle was already there, rearranging her army of stuffed animals.

"You know what?" Michelle said as Stephanie came in. "I'd really like to go on a field trip."

"Me too, Michelle," Stephanie said grimly.

"But what *is* a field trip?" Michelle asked, looking a little confused. "What do you do in the field?"

"Well, it's not necessarily in a field," Stephanie tried to explain. "In this case it's in the woods. And we'll all sleep in tents."

"Wow! That sounds like fun," Michelle said.

"It *is* fun," Stephanie said. "And if I don't get to go, I'll be the most miserable, left-out girl in America!"

"So what did you guys buy at the mall?" Stephanie asked as she sat with Darcy, Allie, and Hilary at lunch the next day.

"None of the boring stuff that's on Mrs. Walker's list," Darcy said with a laugh. "Cool stuff only. I got the greatest backpack, Steph. It's neon green, with silver zigzags on it that glow in the dark."

"And I got some yellow sunglasses and a jean jacket," Allie said. "And Hilary got this fantastic sleeping bag, with pictures of rock stars all over it."

"I bought a Ouija board too," Hilary said. "We can tell our fortunes." She stood up. "I'm going to get another carton of juice. Does anyone want anything?"

Everyone shook their heads. After Hilary left the table, Allie said, "The Ouija board's a great idea, isn't it? Hilary's bringing a book of ghost stories too, so we can read them out loud and scare ourselves to death!"

"It'll be fantastic," Stephanie agreed. "If I get to go, that is."

"Your dad's still trying to decide?" Darcy asked.

Stephanie nodded glumly. "He says he wants to keep an eye on me for a couple of days to make sure I'm perfectly healthy."

"You look fine to me." Allie pointed to Stephanie's empty lunch tray. "And look, you ate every last bite of your lunch, even the limp green beans."

Darcy grinned. "Maybe you *are* still sick, Steph!"

Stephanie laughed. "I'm just making up for all those crackers and Jell-O. Hey, listen," she said. "Why don't you guys come over this weekend and help me persuade Dad? You could drop a few comments like how well I look and how hard I played volleyball in gym."

"Oh, I can't," Darcy said. "Hilary invited me to visit her aunt down in Carmel. We're leaving tomorrow and coming back late Sunday night. Hilary says her aunt's house is right on the water, and you can wake up in the morning and see seals flopping around on the rocks."

"I wish I *could* come over to your house," Allie said to Stephanie. "But my mom's best friend from high school is having a reunion in San Jose and I have to go. I won't know a single person there. It'll be a major bore!"

Talk about a major bore, Stephanie thought. *That's what my weekend is going to be. And what about next weekend? If I'm stuck at home while my entire class is on the camping trip, it won't be just a bore. It'll be a catastrophe!*

Stephanie was startled out of her thoughts by a loud burst of laughter from the next table. Glancing over, she saw Mia waving a French fry around. Suddenly the French fry shot out of Mia's fingers, zoomed through the air, and landed on top of Stephanie's head.

"Sorry, Steph!" Mia hollered as the kids at her table laughed even louder.

"Mia's at it again," Stephanie muttered, picking the potato out of her hair. "First she gets me in trouble in science and now she's tossing food around like a total juvenile. What's with her, anyway?"

"I don't know," Darcy said. "Somebody ought to tell her what a pain she can be."

"Hey, guess what?" Hilary said excitedly as she came back with her juice. "I was talking to some other kids and they said Mrs. Walker posted almost all the tentmates! So I ran to the science room and checked. And . . ." she paused dramatically.

"And?" Allie asked. "Come on, Hilary, don't keep us in suspense."

"We're together!" Hilary said. "You and Darcy and I!"

Stephanie's heart sank. Her two best friends would be sharing a tent with somebody else.

Allie shot Stephanie a sympathetic smile. "I really wish you were going to be with us," she said. "I guess you weren't on the list because you haven't turned in your permission slip yet."

"But listen, we'll try to make sure our tent is next to yours," Darcy said. "That'll be almost the same."

"Sure!" Hilary said. "And you can hang out in our tent at night and tell fortunes and ghost stories and stuff with us. You'll only have to sleep in yours."

"Right." Stephanie forced a smile. "That'll be great."

CHAPTER 3

"Hey, D.J.," Stephanie said on Friday evening, "need some help?" She walked over to her older sister, who was standing by the grill, and started to lift a patty onto the fire. The extended Tanner family—all nine of them—was having a cookout in the backyard, and that meant a lot of burgers.

"Hold on, Steph," Danny said. "D.J.'s doing the hamburgers."

"I'm just going to help her," Stephanie said. "I never get to cook on the grill."

"That's because you're not old enough." D.J. took the spatula from Stephanie's hand.

"That's ridiculous." Stephanie frowned.

"I'm afraid D.J.'s right," Danny said, checking the flames. "You're still too young to cook on the grill. Sometimes the wind blows the flames up pretty high and it can be dangerous. Why don't you help Michelle set the table?"

Stephanie couldn't believe it. *I'm in seventh grade and Dad still treats me like I'm Michelle's age,* she thought. *D.J. gets to do everything she wants, just because she's a senior. I'd give anything to trade places with her.*

"I promise I'll be careful," she pleaded to her father.

"Sorry, honey, but it's too windy tonight," Danny said. "I don't want you to get hurt."

Stephanie loved her dad like crazy, but sometimes his overprotectiveness really got on her nerves. It wasn't just the camping trip, either. It was everything. *I'm surprised he even lets me go to school by myself,* she thought. *Walking down those halls can be dangerous. You never know when a book could fall out of someone's locker and knock you unconscious!*

"Stephanie, can you help me find some rocks?" Michelle asked.

"What do you need rocks for?"

"Every time I put one of those paper plates on the table, it blows away," Michelle said, looking exasperated.

"Ask Nicky and Alex to help you." Stephanie sighed. She looked over at her little nephews, who were running around the backyard trying to catch Comet, the family's golden retriever, by the tail. Uncle Jesse was playing his guitar, and Joey was trying to make Becky laugh with his latest jokes.

"What's that song you're working on?" Becky asked Jesse. "It's new, isn't it?"

Jesse stood up with his guitar, smoothed back his hair, and struck his best Elvis pose. "It's a new song I'm writing for Nicky and Alex." He strummed a few chords, then started to sing.

Every night before I go to sleep
There's one thing I need to keep
in my mind, all the time—
Mommy and Daddy get real tired
So I have to close my eyes
and not be wired!

"No offense, honey, but that's a pretty bad song," Becky said.

"Yeah, I'm afraid she's right," Joey agreed. "I hope you're not planning on doing it with your band."

"Thanks for your support, guys," Jesse said. "And no, I'm not doing it with the band. It's just a little song for the twins."

"So they didn't let you get enough sleep last night?" Stephanie asked.

"Sleep?" Jesse said. "What's that? I think I've forgotten the meaning of the word."

"I remember when the girls kept me up at night," Danny said, getting that dewy-eyed look he always got whenever he talked about Stephanie and her sisters as babies. "Stephanie was the worst. As soon as we thought she'd fallen asleep, we'd hear a scream coming from her room. She wanted to be held all the time."

D.J. pinched Stephanie on the cheek and made a sympathetic face. "Did little Stephie want to be held all the time by her daddy?" she asked in a baby voice.

"Cut it out," Stephanie said hotly. The truth

was that her dad still saw her as that little baby and she didn't think it was funny!

"Okay, everybody," Danny said, walking to the picnic table with a tray full of hamburgers. "Let's eat!"

Everyone crowded around the table, and Danny put a burger on each plate.

"Dad, what's this on my patty?" Stephanie asked.

"It's a happy face," Danny said proudly.

"I know it's a happy face," Stephanie said, looking down at the mustard drawing, "but what's it doing on my hamburger?"

"I thought you'd like it." Danny looked a little disappointed.

"Michelle's the one who likes happy faces," Stephanie pointed out. "I outgrew them about seven years ago."

"I'll switch with you," Michelle offered. "I have a little ducky on mine."

"Thanks, but I'll stick with this one," Stephanie said. She mushed the happy face with her hamburger roll and then took a big bite.

"I bet that tastes good after all the bland food

you've been eating for the last two weeks," Becky said to Stephanie.

Stephanie nodded enthusiastically. "It sure does!" she said, swallowing. "I practically gobbled my lunch today at school, too. My appetite's definitely back. That's a sign of good health, right?"

"Hint, hint," D.J. said. "Dad, in her not-so-subtle way Stephanie's trying to convince you to let her go on the camping trip."

Danny just smiled and said, "Please pass the ketchup, Becky."

"My seventh-grade camp-out was a blast," D.J. went on. "All the girls got together and raided the guys' tents. After that, we all went for a midnight swim."

"A midnight swim?" Danny said, looking concerned. "That wouldn't be a good idea at all, especially for someone who's recovering from the flu."

"*Recovered,*" Stephanie said. "The flu is history."

"I remember a school camping trip I went on," Jesse said. "It was in the mountains, and even though it was May, it started snowing. Everybody was so cold, we put on every piece of clothing we'd brought and we still couldn't get warm enough to go to sleep."

Danny looked even more concerned.

"*This* camping trip isn't in the mountains," Stephanie said. "It's in a state park, remember, Dad? Hills, but no mountains."

"Cold is nothing," Joey chimed in. "On my high school trip, our campsite was invaded by raccoons. Those little critters ate all the food except for the marshmallows. For two days we had to survive on marshmallows and water. That's roughing it!"

Now Danny looked totally worried, and Stephanie started to feel desperate. "I survived two *weeks* on crackers and Jell-O!" she said. "And look at me—I'm fine!"

But Danny just shook his head. "Give it a day or two, Steph," he said. "I know how much you want to go, but I have to be sure you're up to it. Try to understand."

Stephanie started to argue, but then she decided not to. Not yet, anyway. She'd save it. And if arguing didn't work, then she'd pull out all the stops and *beg!*

* * *

"That guy is so cute," Stephanie said. "And he has a great voice." She was watching MTV in the living room with D.J. late that night. It was a live performance of one of Stephanie's favorite rock stars, Eddie Vedder, and she'd been looking forward to watching it all week.

"He is pretty cute," D.J. agreed.

"This is my favorite song of his," Stephanie said, turning up the volume with the remote control. Stephanie was singing along with the television when Danny walked in the room.

"Stephanie, I think you ought to be getting to bed." He picked up the remote control from the coffee table and turned down the volume.

"But the show just started," Stephanie protested. "Besides, it's Friday night.'"

"Sorry, but you really shouldn't be up this late," Danny said. "When you're still getting over the flu, you need your sleep more than ever."

I'm not getting *over the flu!* Stephanie wanted to shout. *I'm* over *it!* "But I can sleep late in the morning," she said.

"In the morning you and D.J. have to be at the dentist's at nine o'clock to have your teeth cleaned," Danny reminded her. "That means getting up at eight."

"Then how come D.J. gets to stay up?" Stephanie asked, totally exasperated.

"Because she hasn't been sick," Danny said. "And because she's older. Now come on, Steph. Time for bed."

"If I hear that D.J.'s older than me one more time, I'm going to scream," Stephanie said.

"Then I guess we'd all better buy earplugs," Danny said with a grin.

This isn't fair, Stephanie thought as she marched out of the living room and up the stairs. *Dad's convinced I'm still a baby. I have to show him I'm not, and the only way to do it is to go on that camping trip!*

CHAPTER 4

◆ ◀ ■ ◆

Stephanie was still mad as she sat in the dentist's waiting room with D.J. on Saturday morning. She picked up a magazine, started to leaf through it, then tossed it down with a loud sigh.

"That's the fourth magazine you haven't looked at," D.J. said. "What's your problem?"

"Dad's my problem," Stephanie said, getting right to the point. "He thinks I'm still a baby."

"You mean because he wouldn't let you stay up late last night?"

"That's part of it," Stephanie said. "But mostly it's the camping trip. I'm really afraid he's not going to let me go."

"He's worried about you since you've been sick," D.J. said, tossing her long brown hair to the side. "After all, you had the flu. You weren't even interested in eating pizza or ice cream—now, that's sick!"

"Well, I'm tired of him worrying about me so much," Stephanie complained. "He'll probably be worrying about me when I'm twenty years old."

"That's just the way he is," D.J. said. "He loves us so much, and he doesn't want anything bad to happen to us. He's always going to be that way, and there's no use trying to change him. It used to bother me, too. Sometimes it still does, but you get used to it." She laughed. "Did I ever tell you what he did the first time I spent the night away from our house?"

"No, I don't think so," Stephanie said.

"Well, I was going to sleep over at Kimmy's," D.J. said. Kimmy was her best friend. "And I'd just finished dinner with her and her parents when the doorbell rang."

"Don't tell me—it was Dad."

"Exactly," D.J. said, laughing again. "He made up this dumb excuse about how he had to take me home because there was some kind of family emergency. Later, he told me he'd just been nervous about me staying away from him for a night."

"Usually it's the other way around," Stephanie said. "I mean, like the first time I stayed over at a friend's, I told her parents I was sick and wanted to go home because I was afraid to be away from Dad." She sighed. "But I'm not afraid to be away from him now. He just doesn't understand that I'm not a little kid anymore."

"I know, but he means well," D.J. said.

"That's easy for you to say. He doesn't treat *you* like a baby," Stephanie said. "You get to do whatever you want."

"That's not true," D.J. said. "I still have a strict curfew. Sometimes Dad's rules bug me, but there's no use fighting them. You should feel lucky that I'm the oldest."

"Why would that ever make me feel lucky?" Stephanie asked in disbelief. "I'm too young to do the stuff you get to do. I can't even cook on the grill. And I'm too old to be treated like Michelle. I mean, she might have to set the table once in a while, but I have *real* chores, like feeding Comet every morning and every night. I'd give anything to be the oldest instead of in the middle."

"That's because you don't know what it's really like," D.J. said. "I've paved the way for you. Everybody knows that parents are always stricter with the oldest."

"Maybe," Stephanie said doubtfully.

"Look, I know Dad's a little protective, but—"

"A *little?*" Stephanie interrupted. "He's superprotective. And D.J., I will seriously have to change schools if I can't go on this class trip. Everybody'll think I'm a dweeb." *And Allie and Darcy probably won't even miss me,* she thought. *They'll be having so much fun with Hilary, they won't even think about me.*

In spite of trying to push her feelings away, Stephanie couldn't help being a little jealous of Hilary.

"Listen," D.J. said, "why don't you start thinking about a plan to get Dad to change his mind?"

"Like what kind of plan?" Stephanie asked.

"Well, what's the reason he might not let you go?"

"You know why," Stephanie said. "I was sick, and he thinks I might not be well enough to go."

"Exactly," D.J. said as if she were Sherlock Holmes explaining a murder mystery. "So all you have to do is prove to him that you're not sick anymore."

Stephanie leaned back in her chair and thought a moment. "Hmmm," she said. "Prove it. You know, I've got a couple of ideas that just might work. Thanks, Deej!"

D.J. grinned. "That's what older sisters are for!"

"Where have you been, Stephanie?" Becky asked when Stephanie walked through the front door later that afternoon. Becky was sitting in the living room playing with the twins, and Danny was folding laundry.

Putting my plan into action, Stephanie thought, taking off her Walkman. "Jogging," she said.

"Your face is bright red." Danny jumped up from the couch and walked over to her. He put one hand on her forehead and the other on his own. "You're burning up. Maybe you should go to bed."

"Relax, Dad," Stephanie said. "I never felt better in my life."

"You're really well enough to jog?" Danny asked. "Didn't you get tired?"

"No, it was great," Stephanie said as enthusiastically as possible. "It's a beautiful day. I love jogging. In fact, I think I'm going to start jogging every day."

"I jog," Joey said as he walked in from the kitchen.

"Really? I never noticed you going jogging," Becky told him. "Come to think of it, I've never seen you do any exercise at all."

"I jog once every six months," Joey said proudly as he picked Nicky up and tossed him in the air. "Anything more than that is excessive. That's how I stay in such great shape."

Stephanie rolled her eyes. "Well, I'm jogging every day from now on," she announced.

"You did a great job with the twins this afternoon, Steph," Becky said. "They were in a wonderful mood when they came back from their outing with you."

"What outing?" Danny asked.

"Stephanie pushed the twins in their stroller

to the park," Becky explained as she rolled a toy car to Nicky, who immediately rolled it back to her.

"But that's a long walk," Danny said. "And with that double stroller—Steph, honey, weren't you exhausted after that?"

"Not the least little bit," Stephanie said as peppily as she could. "In fact, right after D.J. and I got back from the dentist, I washed and vacuumed your car."

"I think we should take your temperature." Danny shook his head. "You could have caused a relapse. I feel like I need a nap myself just from hearing everything you've been doing."

"Dad, I'm feeling fantastic," Stephanie said energetically. "In fact, I'm going upstairs to do fifty sit-ups right now!"

Stephanie ran up the stairs, and even though she was out of breath and completely exhausted, she was feeling triumphant. *I think my plan is going to work,* she thought. *Now he'll have to let me go on the trip!*

"Will you play stuffed animals with me?" Michelle asked Stephanie on Sunday night. They were lying in their beds in the room they shared with each other. One of Michelle's favorite activities was making up different voices for each stuffed animal and acting out little stories.

Even though Stephanie's bedtime was later than Michelle's, she decided to go to bed early that night. She wanted to show her dad that she was getting as much sleep as possible. Besides, she was wiped out. Today she'd done more sit-ups, jogged again, played tag with the twins, mowed the backyard, and mopped the kitchen floor after dinner.

"Not now, Michelle," Stephanie said. There were times that she'd play with Michelle even when she didn't feel like it. Sometimes it was easier to just give in. But right now, she was too tired. And too worried about the camping trip. Danny still hadn't said yes, and time was running out.

"Please," Michelle pleaded. "Pretty please with sugar on top? We'll just do one story." Michelle went over to the chair, picked up Stephanie's teddy bear, and handed him to Stephanie. "Teddy wants to play with Peaches the panda."

"Teddy's just going to have to be upset tonight," Stephanie said. She gave him a hug and put him under the covers with her.

Danny opened their door, and Michelle went running back to her bed. "You should be asleep, Michelle," he said, leaning down to kiss her on the cheek. "It's getting late."

"Okay. Good night, Daddy," Michelle said.

"How are you feeling?" he asked Stephanie as he sat down on her bed.

"I feel great," Stephanie said.

"Well, I've made a decision about your trip," he said.

Stephanie was so nervous, part of her was afraid to hear what his decision was. She took a deep breath and held it. *Please say I can go,* she pleaded silently, and crossed her fingers.

"I think you're over your sickness and you're well enough to go."

Stephanie threw her arms around her dad and gave him a big hug. "You're the best dad in the world! You have no idea how happy I am! I have to go call Allie and Darcy and tell them the news! Wait, I can't—they both said they'd be getting back late. Well, I should start packing right now! And there's some stuff I need to get. I'll go down the list and see what—''

''Wait, slow down, honey,'' Danny said, smiling broadly. ''You're going to have another reason to be happy. I've made another decision as well.''

''Really? What is it?'' Stephanie was hoping he was going to say he decided to take her shopping for a new sleeping bag. *Maybe I'll get one with rock stars on it like Hilary has,* she thought excitedly.

''I've come up with a plan that will solve all our problems,'' Danny started to explain. ''In the letter your teacher sent home, she asked for parents to volunteer to come on the trip as chaperones. Remember?''

''Uh-huh, so?'' Stephanie asked distractedly. Now that she had the news, she couldn't wait to start packing.

''Well, it seems that a chaperone had to quit at the last moment,'' Danny said excitedly. ''Which is just perfect, really, because now I can go on the trip with you!''

CHAPTER 5

"That's really terrific that your dad's going on your camping trip," Jesse said to Stephanie at breakfast on Monday morning.

"I know," Stephanie said, forcing a smile. "It's really nice that he's helping out the class like that."

Secretly, Stephanie was mortified that he was going on the trip with her. Now he'd be hovering over her in front of the entire class! But he was so excited about it that Stephanie didn't want to burst his bubble. Besides, he might not let her go if he didn't go, too. And nothing—not even a super-protective father—would keep her from going.

"I can't wait," Danny said as he placed a platter of waffles on the table. "I've been wanting to get out of the city for a while. And I love camping."

"For some reason I can't imagine you camping out in the wilderness," Becky said, cutting Nicky and Alex's waffles into little pieces.

"Why is that?" Danny asked.

"Well, I just can't picture you with all that dirt around you," Becky said, holding back a giggle.

Danny was totally obsessed with cleanliness. There was nothing he liked better than buying new cleaning products at the store. His idea of a great way to spend the afternoon was to reorganize a closet or scrub the kitchen sink.

"And don't forget about the bugs that will be crawling all around at night," D.J. said.

"Knowing Danny, he'll probably bring along his Dustbuster and try to clear away all the pine needles in the forest," Joey teased.

"Very funny," Danny said. "The fact of the matter is that I happen to be a great outdoorsman. When I was a Boy Scout, I used to go camping almost once a month."

"That was only a hundred years ago," Joey said.

"I guess I should remind you that you're exactly the same age as I am, old man," Danny said.

"Dad, do you think it would be okay if I came, too?" Michelle asked. "We could all share a tent together!"

Everybody laughed except Stephanie. *Why doesn't the whole family come along,* she thought as she poured syrup on her waffles. *We could call it the Tanner Family Expedition. Then I could really be humiliated in front of my entire class.*

"Guess what?" Stephanie said as she hurried down the hall toward Allie and Darcy later that morning. "Dad said yes! I'm going on the camping trip!"

"That's great!" Allie cried excitedly. "I just knew he wouldn't let you miss it."

"Me, too," Darcy said with a big grin. "He's pretty cool for a father."

"I'm glad you think so, because he's coming along," Stephanie said. "He volunteered to be one of the chaperones. I just hope he doesn't embarrass me in front of everybody by taking my temperature every ten minutes or something like that."

"Yeah, I know what you mean," Allie said. "My dad's the same way sometimes. But the main thing is you're going, right? Now we can have our tents next to each other and play with the Ouija board together and stuff. It's going to be so much fun. I'm really getting psyched!"

"Yeah," Stephanie said happily. "And Dad's taking me to the mall after school today so I can buy a bunch of things. Why don't you guys come, too?"

"Today?" Darcy said. "Actually, Allie and I are going over to Hilary's after school today. Since we're in the same tent, we decided to get together and make a list of stuff to bring."

"Junk food and magazines and things like that," Allie explained. "But I could go shopping tomorrow. What about you, Darcy?"

"Sure."

Stephanie shook her head. "Today's the only day Dad can get to the mall," she said. "And I've still got a pile of makeup work to do, plus the normal homework, so I'm going to be working like crazy the rest of the week."

Stephanie couldn't help feeling another little twinge of jealousy. While she was shopping with her father, her two best friends would be having a great time with Hilary.

"Well, anyway, we'll spend lots of time together on the trip," Darcy said. "I'm so glad you get to go, Steph!"

"Me, too," Stephanie agreed. She pushed the jealous feeling to the back of her mind. *You're going on the trip,* she told herself. *That's the most important thing.*

"I stopped at the drugstore on the way home today and bought some extra-strong insect repellant," Danny said, walking into Stephanie and Michelle's bedroom. It was Wednesday night and Stephanie was packing her duffel bag and backpack for the trip.

"Thanks, Dad." Stephanie took the can.

"The man at the store told me that's the best kind on the market these days," he said proudly. "Apparently this is what conservationists use when they're hiking in the Amazon rain forest."

"Great. I'm sure I'll make it through the weekend without a single mosquito bite."

"You have to make sure that you put it on all over you the second you get up in the morning," Danny instructed. "You also want to put it on top of your head, because that's where the mosquitoes gravitate. Just be careful to keep it out of your eyes, and most importantly, keep it out of your mouth."

"Okay, Dad. I will."

Danny left her room, and Stephanie checked off different items on her list as she put them in the duffel bag. She was really starting to get excited now. She didn't even mind it when Hilary joined Darcy, Allie, and her for lunch. *If only I knew who* my *tentmates will be,* she thought. Mrs. Walker had said she'd be making the final assignments when they arrived at the campsite. Stephanie hoped she'd be with kids she liked.

Five minutes later Danny came back carrying a pair of hiking boots. "These were D.J.'s boots," he said. "I bought them for her when she went on her seventh-grade camp-out. I just got through cleaning and brushing them, and I put some special waterproof treatment on them so they won't get ruined if it rains."

Stephanie eyed the huge, clunky boots he was holding. They were an ugly brown color, with enormous rubber soles and yellow laces, and they looked like they were for serious hikers. She was sure nobody else would be wearing anything so uncool. "Thanks, Dad," she said, "but I thought I'd just wear sneakers."

"Sneakers?" Danny's jaw dropped open.

"Yeah, I don't need such heavy-duty boots. We're just going for two nights, and we'll be doing very light hiking. It's not like we're going mountain climbing or anything."

"You can't wear sneakers," Danny said. "You could slip on wet leaves and fall down. You can't take the risk of twisting your ankle. Also, it's bad for your feet to hike without the right kind of support."

Stephanie took a deep breath and told herself to stay calm. *Just take the boots and don't make a scene,* she advised herself. The boots were obviously important to her dad, so she decided just to grin and bear it. "Okay, Dad, I'll bring the boots. Thanks a lot."

"My pleasure," he said, leaving the room.

Stephanie sighed. *We're not even on the trip yet and he's already treating me like a little girl,* she thought. *But I can't let him get to me.*

"What are you doing?" Michelle asked as she walked through the door.

"I'm packing for my trip," Stephanie replied. "There's a lot of stuff on this list I have to take with me."

"Aren't you going to take Teddy?"

Stephanie looked over at the chair where her teddy bear was sitting. He looked sort of sad and neglected. Stephanie *would* have liked to take her teddy bear with her. She'd slept with him almost every night of her life. And even though she was totally thrilled about going on the trip, she was just a teeny bit nervous. She'd never slept outside in the woods before. She wasn't afraid of bears or anything, but she was a little afraid of the woods at night. Still, there was no way she'd pack Teddy. It would be way too embarrassing if anyone saw him.

"Teddy's going to have to stay here," Stephanie said. "I'm too old to take him with me. Will you take care of him for me while I'm gone?"

"You can count on me," Michelle said, obviously excited to be given such an important responsibility. "I'll let him sleep in my bed, and I'll say nice things to him so he won't miss you too much."

"Thanks, Michelle. I'll feel better knowing I'm leaving him in safe hands."

"Steph, I just put new batteries in this flashlight," Danny said, coming into her room for practically the tenth time that night. "I'm also giving you extra batteries in case these wear out."

"Thanks." Stephanie sighed. The flashlight was enormous, and she didn't know how she'd manage to fit it into her duffel bag.

"It's waterproof, so even if you drop it on the ground, it still works." Danny was beaming. It was amazing to Stephanie that he could get so excited about something as silly as a flashlight.

"Wow, it really sounds great, Dad," Stephanie said, trying to match his excitement. She couldn't imagine that she would even need a flashlight, but there was no point in telling her father that.

"I thought that in case you got scared in your

tent at night, you could keep this on as a night-light,'' Danny said.

He really does think I'm a baby, Stephanie thought. Then she had a thought that made her feel better. *Maybe since he'll be on the trip, he'll see for himself that I'm more grown up than he realizes.*

CHAPTER 6

Stephanie was so excited on Saturday morning that she couldn't even eat her breakfast. Last night as she was falling asleep she'd decided that she would just pretend her father wasn't even on the trip with her. She figured there'd be so many activities going on and people around that they wouldn't even have to come in contact with each other that much.

"Steph, you've barely touched your French toast," Danny said. "That's usually your favorite breakfast. You're not getting sick again, are you?"

"Not at all," Stephanie reassured him. "I guess I'm just too excited to eat."

"Well, you need your energy if you're going to be doing physical activity on the trip today, so eat up," Danny said.

Stephanie forced herself to eat her French toast even though she wasn't hungry. If eating proved she was well enough to go on the trip, she'd stuff herself!

"Do you think we could have a camping trip in our backyard when you come home?" Michelle asked Stephanie.

"Absolutely," Stephanie said. "By then, I'll be an expert camper."

Danny looked at his watch and jumped up from the table. "We should get going. We don't want to miss that bus."

"You're lucky you get to go camping," Michelle said when Stephanie was about to leave. "I wish I was old enough to go."

"I know just how you feel, Michelle," Stephanie said, giving her a good-bye kiss on the cheek.

It seemed to Stephanie that her dad was driving slower than usual as they made their way to Stephanie's school to meet the bus and that they kept hitting every red light. She couldn't wait to be on the bus with her friends.

"Honey, I want you to be sure and bundle up warmly at night," Danny advised. "I packed some extra long underwear in your bag."

Great. I wonder what else he packed that I don't know about, she thought. *I'll be surprised if he didn't pack my bed so I'll sleep comfortably at night.*

"Okay," Stephanie said. "I promise to dress warmly."

"Also, I want you to stay with somebody else at all times," he instructed. "Don't go wandering off by yourself for even a moment."

"I'm sure that won't be a problem since the class will probably stay together except for when we're in our tents at night," Stephanie said.

"I brought along some antihistamines in case you get an allergy to anything," he said. "If your eyes start itching or your nose starts running, just let me know."

"But I don't have allergies," Stephanie pointed out.

"You never know," Danny said. "You can develop new allergies at any time in your life. There might be some plants around that you've never been exposed to before. And that reminds me of something else."

"Yes?" Stephanie asked. "What does that remind you of?"

"I packed some calamine lotion in your bag in case you come in contact with poison ivy," Danny said. "You know what poison ivy looks like, don't you?"

"Yes, Dad." Stephanie sighed heavily. "Our science teacher showed us pictures of poison ivy in class. It has three leaves and little white flowers."

"Right. So when you're hiking, be sure to wear long pants and socks—then your legs won't brush against it."

"Okay, Dad."

"Now, Stephanie, I want you to remember a few safety tips when you're on this trip," Danny said in a concerned voice.

"Okay, what?" Stephanie asked impatiently.

"Well, for one thing, you shouldn't keep any food in your tent," Danny said. "That could attract animals and bugs."

"What kind of animals?" Stephanie asked, looking over at her father.

"Raccoons, squirrels, bears—"

"Bears? Are you serious? Are there really bears in those woods where we're going?"

"Just kidding about the bears," Danny said, chuckling to himself. "I just wanted to keep you on your toes."

"That's a relief," Stephanie said, laughing.

"Hey, guys!" Stephanie shouted as she ran up to Darcy and Allie in the school parking lot. "I thought I'd never make it here."

Stephanie felt a wave of excitement as she saw the whole class moving around the bus in a flurry of activity. A group of students was throwing around a Frisbee, and another group was tossing a football back and forth. There was a huge pile of backpacks and tents on the ground, and parents were shouting last-minute advice to their kids.

"We were starting to get worried that you weren't coming," Allie said.

"Are you kidding?" Stephanie said. "I wouldn't miss this trip for anything."

"I brought a deck of cards for tonight," Darcy

said. "My cousin taught me how to do some cool tricks that I thought I could show you guys."

"That sounds great," Stephanie said.

"I brought some chocolate chip cookies that I made last night," Allie said. "I thought we could eat them while we're telling ghost stories so we wouldn't be so scared."

"Yummy," Darcy said. "My favorite."

Stephanie remembered her dad's warning about keeping food in the tent, but she reasoned that a few cookies wouldn't hurt. She looked over at her dad, who was busily organizing the boxes of food, duffel bags, and tents in the bottom compartment of the bus. He looked so happy to be helping out on the trip that Stephanie had a momentary guilty pang when she remembered how upset she'd been about his coming. *It's sweet that he wanted to come along,* she thought. Stephanie was shaken from her thoughts when she heard loud music.

"Look at Mia," Stephanie said. "She's bringing along her gigantic boom box with a CD player in it."

"That's the dumbest thing I've ever seen," Allie said. "I don't see what that has to do with appreciating nature. And her poor tentmates are never going to get to sleep if she blasts music all night."

"And look what she's wearing," Darcy commented. "She looks like she's going to a birthday party, not on a camping trip." Stephanie and her friends all looked at Mia, who was wearing a fancy pair of linen shorts with a matching vest and clogs.

"How's she going to hike in those shoes?" Darcy said.

"At least her dad didn't force her to bring a pair of clunky hiking boots," Stephanie said. "You should see the ones my father made me bring! They probably weigh as much as Mia's boom box." She rolled her eyes. "And he's been giving me so many instructions, I feel like I'm going camping for two years instead of two days."

"At least you're going camping," Allie said. "Anyway, don't worry about your dad. He's pretty cool compared to a lot of parents."

"Yeah, I hope so," Stephanie said to herself as she bounded up the stairs and into the bus.

* * *

"That was great, everybody. Now let's sing the song about the bus. That's one of Stephanie's favorites." Danny was standing at the front of the bus, leading the class in a sing-along. Everyone seemed to be having a great time singing. Everyone except Stephanie.

Stephanie was slouched down in her seat next to Darcy. Allie and Hilary were sitting in the seats in front of them. Stephanie was totally embarrassed by her dad. He looked like he was having a blast. She knew he wouldn't understand why she wasn't thrilled to have him provide entertainment for her whole class. *Why can't he just sit quietly in the front with the other chaperones and teachers?* she wondered.

"Why aren't you singing?" Darcy asked. "You have a great voice."

"I guess I'm just not in the mood," Stephanie said, sliding farther down in her seat.

"But your dad said this was your favorite song," Allie said.

"It *was*, when I was five years old." The class was applauding their last song, and Danny had a huge grin on his face.

"Now let's do the one about talking to the

animals, from *Dr. Doolittle,*'' Danny said excitedly. ''Stephanie has loved that movie since she was really little.''

I'm surprised he doesn't take out baby pictures of me and pass them around the bus, Stephanie thought miserably.

CHAPTER 7

"Isn't it beautiful here?" Darcy said. "Look at all those trees!"

Stephanie nodded. "It's great to be out of the city for a change," she said, looking around. She and the rest of the class were sitting in a big clearing next to a lake. Beyond the clearing were gently rolling tree-covered hills with rushing streams and paths for hiking.

Stephanie was thrilled to have finally arrived at the campsite. Everyone was talking and laughing excitedly in anticipation of the next couple of days. *I didn't think that bus ride would ever end,* Stephanie thought. *Thank goodness Dad's musical entertainment is over!*

"All right, everybody," Mrs. Walker said to the class. "The first thing we need to do is pitch the tents." She paused as a loud burst of rock music almost drowned out her voice. "Mia! Please turn that thing off!" she said sternly.

Everyone looked at Mia, who grinned and turned off her boom box.

"We're here for a nature trip," Mrs. Walker said. "Listen to the sounds around you—bird calls, the babbling of the brook in the woods."

"And the growling of the bears," Allie whispered. "They're saying, 'I'm hungry. Look at all those seventh graders. Yummy, yummy!' "

Stephanie giggled.

"Cut it out, Allie," Darcy said, giving her a friendly shove. "You know I'm afraid of bears. And my dad said there aren't any bears here anyway."

"Most of you already know who your tent partners are," Mrs. Walker went on, "but those who don't should listen closely while I read off the names. We have eleven tents and thirty-two students, so there will be ten tents with three people in each and one tent with two people."

As Mrs. Walker started reading off names,

Stephanie crossed her fingers that she'd be in a tent with someone she liked. While she was waiting to hear her name, she looked over to see what her father was doing.

Danny was sitting off to the side of the clearing, scraping mud off his shoes. After he'd finished scraping, he took out some Handi Wipes and started polishing the tops of the shoes. *Handi Wipes,* Stephanie thought, shaking her head and smiling. *He sure comes prepared!*

Mrs. Walker was still calling off names, but she hadn't said Stephanie's yet. Stephanie hadn't been paying enough attention to see who else hadn't been called. *Please let me be with people I like,* she pleaded silently. *Who could it be?*

Stephanie glanced around the group and wondered who was left. She looked at Allie, and they both exchanged puzzled glances and shrugs.

"And finally," Mrs. Walker said, "Stephanie will be sharing a tent with Mia."

Half an hour later Stephanie and Mia ducked through the flap of their bright orange tent and looked around. "Whoa!" Mia said, putting her hand on her hip. "Not exactly roomy, is it?" The sides of the tent sloped to the ground, and the only place they could stand up straight was in the middle. "We're lucky we don't have to share this with a third person."

"Yeah," Stephanie said. Actually she would have been happy to share it with *five* people, as long as one of them wasn't Mia. All the other kids had laughed and joked while they set up their tents. Mia complained about how hard it was.

Telling herself that the only time she'd really have to spend with Mia was when they were asleep, Stephanie started lugging her camping gear into the tent.

"You sure brought a lot with you," Mia remarked. She sat down on one side of the tent floor and pulled a bottle of nail polish out of her bag. "Looks like enough stuff for two weeks!"

Stephanie shoved her duffel bag to a far corner of the tent, then dragged her sleeping bag inside. The tent flap was made out of some kind of netting, but it wasn't big enough to let in much fresh air. As the fumes of the nail polish wafted through the small space, Stephanie started breathing through her mouth.

"What do you have in that bag, anyway?" Mia asked. "Your entire wardrobe?"

Stephanie looked at Mia's bag, which seemed practically empty. Then she looked at her own, which was overflowing with supplies. Actually she was embarrassed by all the stuff her dad had made her bring, but she wasn't about to tell that to Mia. "I like to be prepared," she said, trying to sound convincing. The smell of the polish was giving her a headache.

"I like to pack light," Mia said, brushing deep plum polish onto her left thumb. "All I brought was a nightshirt, an adorable sundress, my sleeping bag, my boom box, and a bunch of CDs."

"What about stuff like insect repellant, hiking boots, and calamine lotion?" Stephanie asked, unrolling her sleeping bag on one side of the tent. "Didn't your parents make you bring junk like that?"

Mia shook her head. "My mom lets me do whatever I want."

Stephanie thought about her dad and all the

time he'd spent helping her get ready for the trip. She couldn't imagine having a parent who didn't care what she took with her. "I guess my dad's a little overly protective. He stuffed my bag full of equipment."

"Maybe you should join the Girl Scouts," Mia suggested. She waved her fingers in the air to dry the nails. "You like this color?" she asked.

By now Stephanie was almost gagging from the smell. "Yeah, it's great. Gotta go, Mia," she said with a gasp. "See you later!"

Everyone was gathered around the lake, getting ready to go on a canoe trip that afternoon after lunch. People were strapping on their life vests and choosing up canoe partners. Stephanie decided just to push her unhappiness about Mia out of her thoughts. After all, there was nothing she could do about it, and she was excited about going canoeing. She scanned the group to see where her friends were. She breathed a sigh of relief when she spotted Allie waving to her from a distance.

"How's it going with Mia?" Allie asked as she and Darcy and Hilary walked up to Stephanie.

Stephanie glanced over at Mia, who was wearing a purple sundress and sandals and complaining to a bunch of guys about the hot dogs they'd eaten for lunch. "Not great," she said with a sigh. "She practically asphyxiated me with nail polish! If she's brought nail polish *remover,* I'll definitely pass out."

Darcy shook her head. "What did you guys talk about, anyway?"

"Mostly Mia talked about all the stuff I brought," Stephanie said. "Maybe she was trying to be funny, but it got on my nerves. It was the first real conversation I've ever had with her, and I have the terrible feeling it's not going to get much better." She sighed again. "Oh, well, at least I only have to be with her at night. And I'm really glad my tent's next to yours. I hope you don't mind, but I plan to spend a lot of time in it!"

"Of course we don't mind," Allie said.

"Tonight I'll tell your future on the Ouija board," Hilary offered.

"That sounds great," Stephanie said. "I just hope Mia's not part of it."

"Let's all go in this canoe together," Darcy suggested as they walked along the shore of the lake.

Stephanie was just about to climb into the yellow canoe with her friends when Danny came running up.

"Hang on a second, Steph," he said. "I want to make sure you fastened your life jacket correctly." He felt to make sure the straps were tightly fastened. "And I want you to keep it on when you go for a swim."

"Dad, I'm *not* wearing that when I go swimming," Stephanie whispered urgently. "Nobody else will be wearing a life jacket when they swim."

"I don't care what everyone else is wearing. That water is deep, and I don't want to take the chance of you drowning."

"But I'll look like a total dork with that on!" Stephanie said.

"I've taught you your whole life not to worry about what other people think. Your safety is more important than anything else."

"Okay, class," Mrs. Walker said. "I want you

to remember the boating safety rules we went over in class last week."

Stephanie couldn't wait to get in her canoe and away from her dad. *I'm surprised he didn't insist on going in the same canoe with me,* Stephanie thought as she dipped her paddle in the water and pushed away from the shore.

CHAPTER 8

"Wow, talk about a lot of food!" Mia said to Stephanie later that afternoon. "What are we going to do with all of it—open a supermarket?"

After everybody came back from canoeing, Mrs. Walker had assigned each tent a different chore. Stephanie and Mia were put in charge of unpacking the food for the trip. They were taking everything out of boxes and lining it up on picnic tables near the fire, where the food would be cooked that evening.

Darcy, Allie, and Hilary had been assigned to come up with songs to sing at the campfire the next night—something Stephanie would much rather be doing. Other people were in charge of clearing the campsite of trash, and others were collecting discarded bottles to recycle when they got back to school.

"I guess it just takes a lot of food to feed so many people," Stephanie said, putting bags of tortilla chips on the table.

"I suppose so," Mia said. She pulled out some huge cans of tomatoes and thumped them on the table. "What are we going to do with these?"

"Chili," Stephanie said.

Mia wrinkled her nose.

"Don't you like chili?" Stephanie asked.

"It's okay, I guess," Mia said. "It's just kind of boring. Too bad there's not a telephone around here. We could order Chinese takeout."

"Yeah, well, we're in the wilderness, remember?"

"Tell me about it." Mia rolled her eyes. "I couldn't believe that lake. You couldn't even see the bottom!" She shuddered.

Mia was definitely not a happy camper, Stephanie thought.

"Hey, this is more like it!" Mia said, taking

out some chocolate bars. "They'd make a great snack in the tent tonight."

"I know," Stephanie said. "But we're using them to make s'mores after dinner."

"What are s'mores?" Mia asked.

"They're graham crackers with roasted marshmallows and these candy bars in the middle," Stephanie explained. "They're great. Everybody always wants more, so that's why they're called . . ."

"S'mores," Mia said. "I get it. I'm not crazy about marshmallows, though. I'd rather have a plain candy bar."

As Mia and Stephanie continued unpacking food, Stephanie suddenly saw something that made her heart stop. Mia looked all around, then reached into a box and pulled out six large candy bars. She put three in each of her jacket pockets, winked at Stephanie, and walked away.

Stephanie was totally stunned. She'd never seen anyone steal anything before. And she didn't know what to do about it.

"Remember that there are thousands of ecosystems in the forest," Mrs. Walker was saying to the students, who were all sitting at picnic tables before dinner. "Anytime you disturb one animal or plant, you're effecting a whole chain reaction."

Stephanie was sitting at a table with Darcy, Allie, and Hilary, but she was barely listening to a word of Mrs. Walker's nature lecture. All she could think about were the candy bars she'd seen Mia take earlier. She knew she should have said something to her dad or her teacher about it, but she was afraid of what Mia might do.

Stephanie looked at Darcy and Allie. She wanted to tell them about the candy bars, but she hadn't had a chance yet.

"Stephanie, can I see you for a minute?" Mrs. Jacobs, one of the chaperones, asked in an urgent whisper.

"What is it? What's wrong?" Stephanie asked. She looked up at Mrs. Jacobs's face, which was usually warm and friendly. Instead she saw a face that seemed deeply upset about something.

"Just come with me." Mrs. Jacobs led Stephanie to a bench away from the group. Mia was sitting on a big log at the edge of the clearing. She didn't look at Stephanie when she sat down.

"I need to talk to you girls about something important," Mrs. Jacobs said in a concerned voice.

"What is it?" Mia asked.

"I just went into your tent to make sure you'd assembled it correctly, and I saw something that made me very upset." Mrs. Jacobs shook her head.

Stephanie had a sick feeling in her stomach. "What is it? What did you see?"

"I found six candy bars in your tent. Now I can't be sure, but I'm wondering if they came from the food supply for the trip," Mrs. Jacobs said. "I know that you two were in charge of unloading the food this afternoon, so when I saw the candy bars—"

"You assumed we stole them!" Mia snapped.

"I'm not saying you girls stole them. I'm just trying to figure out what happened," Mrs. Jacobs said. "You two unloaded the food, the candy bars were part of our supplies, so it just looks a little suspicious."

Stephanie was speechless. She had never been in a position like this before. Would she get in trouble? What would her father say? She was trying not to cry, but she felt the tears start to well up.

Suddenly Danny came over and asked what was going on. As Mrs. Jacobs explained, Stephanie saw her father's expression change from curiosity to anger.

"Are you accusing my little girl of being a thief?" Danny demanded. "Stephanie would never do a thing like that."

"I'm not accusing her of anything," Mrs. Jacobs said. "I was just asking some questions."

"Dad, I can handle this—" Stephanie began. But her father interrupted.

"Come on, honey, you don't have to stay here and be treated like a criminal," Danny said, putting his arm around Stephanie. "I'll have a little chat with you later," he said to Mrs. Jacobs. "I'm sure my daughter is not involved in this."

Danny led Stephanie away by the hand and said, "Honey, I'm certain—"

"Dad, how could you humiliate me like that?" Stephanie interrupted when they were far enough away from her classmates. "I can stand up for myself!"

"I was just trying to protect you," Danny said, looking confused.

"But you're just making everything worse!" Stephanie cried. "I'm not your little girl anymore and I want you to stop acting like I am!"

Stephanie ran into the woods as fast as she could, leaving her father standing with his mouth open.

"Thanks for not telling on me," Mia said later that night as she and Stephanie were getting ready to go to sleep in their tent.

"Yeah, well, I wish you'd told Mrs. Jacobs I didn't have anything to do with it," Stephanie said as she put on the long underwear her father had packed for her. She'd run through the woods by herself for about twenty minutes after her blowup with her father, and she was exhausted. "Now she thinks I'm a thief," she said. "I mean, you took the candy bars and you got caught. You could have at least kept me out of it."

When Mia didn't say anything, Stephanie turned and looked at her. Mia was sitting on her rolled-up sleeping bag, staring at the ground.

Before Stephanie could say anything else, Mia reached over and turned on her boom box. Loud music blared through the tent.

"Could you please turn off that music? Or at least turn it down?" Stephanie asked. "Mrs. Jacobs will probably come here any minute. We've already been in enough trouble for one day."

"Oh, all right." Mia turned down the sound and scooted off her sleeping bag. Then she unrolled it and crawled inside.

Tired and upset, Stephanie crawled into her own sleeping bag and turned her back to Mia. In the next tent she could hear Allie, Darcy, and Hilary talking and laughing. She'd planned to meet her friends in their tent, but she just wasn't in the mood anymore.

She put her hands over her ears so she wouldn't hear Mia's music or the sounds of her friends having a great time without her.

She snuggled deeper down into her sleeping bag, hoping to block everything out. As she did, something fuzzy brushed against her feet at the bottom of the bag. For a minute she thought it was a squirrel, and it startled her. But when she reached down to see what it was, she realized it was Teddy. She pulled him up to her chest and hugged him tightly, keeping him hidden from Mia. *Thanks, Michelle, for packing Teddy in my sleeping bag,* Stephanie thought. *I need him right now.* Finally, the tears that had been building all day fell slowly down her cheeks and onto Teddy's soft comforting fur.

CHAPTER 9

When Stephanie woke up Sunday morning, she told herself to have a positive attitude. Today just couldn't be as bad as yesterday. This afternoon the class was going on a big hike in the woods. She'd stick with Darcy and Allie and stay as far away from her father and Mia as possible.

But the minute she saw her two friends and Hilary, her positive attitude started to fade. The three of them all had their hair braided exactly the same way. *They're getting to be such good friends,* Stephanie thought, feeling totally left out.

"Why didn't you come by our tent last night?" Darcy asked as Stephanie sat down across from them at the picnic table. "We were waiting for you to hang out with us."

"Yeah, we stuffed ourselves with cookies and told fortunes on my Ouija board," Hilary said, spooning up Cheerios.

"And look what we made," Allie said, holding up her arm.

Around Allie's wrist was a bracelet, braided in strips of bright yellow and orange yarn. Stephanie looked at Darcy's and Hilary's wrists. They were wearing them too. *Friendship bracelets,* she thought miserably.

"So why didn't you come over?" Darcy asked again.

"Why didn't you come get me?" Stephanie asked, a little sharply.

Allie and Darcy exchanged glances. "We looked into your tent," Allie said. "But you and Mia were sound asleep."

"Oh." Stephanie drank some orange juice. "Well, I was really tired."

Darcy and Allie exchanged another glance.

"Okay, Steph, what's wrong?" Darcy said. "We know you too well. You can't keep anything from us."

Stephanie explained the whole horrible story about the candy bars to Allie, Darcy, and Hilary. She told them about how Mia took them, and how she'd even fought with her father.

"I knew Mia was a pain, but I didn't know she was a thief," Darcy said when Stephanie was finished.

"Your real friends know you're not a thief," Allie said.

"Thanks." Stephanie said. She felt better, but not completely. Darcy and Allie were having such a great time without her. She hated feeling jealous of Hilary, but she couldn't help it. "Well, anyway, I'm only stuck with Mia for one more night. And today I won't have to be bothered by her. I can go hiking with you," she said. "We can hang out like we always do. And everything will be back to normal."

But as she looked at her friends with their identical braids and bracelets, she couldn't help wondering if things would *ever* be back to normal.

"Steph, can you come here for a minute?" Danny yelled that afternoon as the class was getting ready for the hike.

Stephanie walked slowly toward where her dad was sitting on a log. *He better not want to talk any more about those chocolate bars,* Stephanie thought.

"I want to spray some bug repellant on you before you go hiking," Danny said, pushing down on the nozzle of the can.

"I can do it myself," Stephanie said. But it was too late. Danny was already spraying her. In fact, he sprayed so much on her that she practically choked.

"Are you okay?" Danny asked as Stephanie was coughing. "Do you want some water?"

"No, Dad," she said between coughs. "I'm just fine."

Danny didn't seem to hear her. "You didn't tie your boots right," he said, leaning down to relace them.

Stephanie looked around and saw that a bunch of students were watching her dad tie her shoes. *How humiliating,* she thought. She heard a couple of people actually snickering. And Hilary was smiling.

Stephanie felt like running into the woods and

never coming back. "Dad, can you cut it out?" she whispered urgently.

"What? What did I do?"

"You're embarrassing me," Stephanie said.

Danny looked back at her with a confused expression.

"What did I do?" he asked again.

But the damage had already been done. "Nothing," Stephanie said, sighing heavily. "Never mind."

"I want you to be careful on the hike," Danny cautioned. "Those woods can get thick and confusing, so you need to pay attention to the path you're going on."

"Okay, Dad," Stephanie said impatiently.

"Do you have your flashlight?"

"It's too heavy; I left it in my tent," Stephanie said. "We're hiking in the daytime, so I don't need a flashlight anyway. Besides, this isn't the Boy Scouts."

"You never know—anything could happen. I always say, 'You're never sorry if you're overly prepared, but you're always sorry if you're not prepared enough.' "

"Dad, it doesn't matter because it's in my tent and I'm not going back for it," Stephanie said.

"Not to worry," he said excitedly. "I have another one right here in my pack."

Danny reached into his pack and pulled out an enormous flashlight exactly like the clunky one Stephanie had left in her tent. Stephanie hoped nobody was watching as he put it in her pack.

Just then, Mrs. Walker started calling everyone to gather together. Relieved, Stephanie ran away from her dad before he could "prepare" her any more.

Stephanie sat with Allie, Darcy, and Hilary at a picnic table as Mrs. Walker gave out last-minute instructions for the hike. It bugged her the way her friends kept giggling and whispering with Hilary about stuff they'd done in their tent the night before. *I hope Hilary doesn't come with us on the hike,* Stephanie thought. She didn't feel like she could say anything to Allie and Darcy about it, though. She didn't want them to know she was jealous.

"Those are pretty serious hiking boots, Stephanie," Hilary said. "Do you do a lot of strenuous outdoor stuff?"

Stephanie wasn't positive, but she thought she detected a slight smirk on Hilary's face. "Not really. They're good for hiking, though. Sneakers don't really give that much support."

"Hilary was telling us that she's getting a trampoline next week," Allie said.

"Yeah, it would be great if the three of you want to come over and try it out," Hilary said, smiling at Stephanie.

"That would be fun," Stephanie said, although it was the last thing she felt like doing.

"Okay, class, listen up!" Mrs. Walker shouted over the excited voices of the students. "There are a lot of different paths in these woods. All of them are clearly marked, but you must pay close attention at all times. It's easy to get lost if you're not careful.

"At the end of the day, we're going to have a sing-along around the campfire and make s'mores. Everybody be sure to collect dry wood for the fire. Stephanie and Mia, you're in charge of gathering sticks to roast the marshmallows. All tent partners will be hiking together, and you'll be going on several different trails. So stick together and don't lose track of your group. Each path winds around and ends up back here."

Stephanie sat straight up on the bench. This couldn't be happening to her. She couldn't believe she was going to have to spend the day hiking with Mia.

"Bummer," Hilary said. "Looks like you're stuck with Mia again, Stephanie."

Stephanie was too upset to speak.

"I guess we better get going," Darcy said. "We'll see you at the campfire, Steph."

"Don't feel too bad," Allie comforted. "We can hang out together at the sing-along."

"Yeah, no problem," Stephanie said, watching her friends walk away.

"Oh, Stephanie, I'm glad I caught you before you left," Danny said, rushing up to her. "I just wanted to take one last look in your pack to make sure you have everything you need."

Stephanie took a step back. "I have *more* than everything I need, Dad," she said through gritted teeth. "Will you please, please, *please* stop worrying about me? I can take care of myself!"

Without waiting for Danny's reaction, Stephanie went off to join Mia.

"I saw your dad tying your shoes for you today," Mia said to Stephanie.

It was the first time either one had spoken since they'd started hiking on the path an hour before, and Stephanie would have preferred that the silence continue.

"Yeah, so, what about it?" Stephanie asked.

"Nothing, I just noticed it. That's all."

Stephanie didn't get the point of her comment, but she didn't really care. She just wanted to keep hiking in peace and quiet. Mia had brought along her boom box on the hike, which Stephanie thought was ridiculous. *It's probably as heavy as this stupid flashlight Dad made me carry.*

As they walked along Stephanie could hear other kids on other trails, laughing and joking. At first she'd been able to see them, too. But now the different paths had become separated by thick forest and she could only hear them. She couldn't see her dad anymore, either. When they'd started out, she'd been positive he'd walk with her and Mia, warning them not to trip on rocks or brush against any strange-looking plants. But he'd stayed with another group, thank goodness. *Maybe he finally got the message that I'm not a little kid anymore,* she thought.

"You know, I can't do all the work here," Stephanie finally said, holding out the sticks she'd been picking up. "Mrs. Walker said for both of us to collect twigs. You haven't picked one up the whole time."

"Yeah, but I've got my boom box to carry," Mia said.

Stephanie was too irritated to even say anything more. She just kept walking.

After a few more minutes Mia sat down on a log. She took off her backpack and set her boom box on a flat rock. "I've got to rest. My feet are absolutely killing me," she said, easing off one of her sneakers. "Look. That blister's the size of a quarter!"

No wonder, Stephanie thought, looking at Mia's old, flimsy sneakers. Stephanie's feet weren't bothering her at all, thanks to the boots her dad had made her wear. "Look, we have to keep going," she said. "We're not supposed to lose track of the rest of the class."

With a groan, Mia put her sneaker back on. But after ten more minutes of walking she stopped to rest again. "My arm feels like it's going to fall off!" she said, setting her boom box on a bed of pine needles and plopping down beside it. "And these mosquitoes are the worst!" she added, smacking one on her leg. "Aren't you getting a lot of bites?"

"Actually, I haven't been bothered by any bugs at all," Stephanie said. She thought about her dad drowning her with repellant and how mad she'd been about it. Now she had to admit to herself that she was glad he'd done it. "Come on, let's go."

With another groan, Mia dragged herself to her feet.

As they kept walking Stephanie noticed that the sounds of the other hikers were fading. She looked around to see if she could spot anyone, but it was impossible to see anything through the thick wall of trees.

After another fifteen minutes Mia collapsed on another fallen log. "I can't go any farther," she said, fanning herself with her hand. "My feet are about to fall off and these mosquitoes are eating me alive. And this boom box weighs a ton!"

"We have to keep going," Stephanie said. "We're supposed to meet up with everybody at the same time. The longer you sit there, the longer it'll take to get back."

Mia didn't budge from her log. Stephanie thought about going along without her, but she decided that she'd rather be with Mia than in the woods all alone. Stephanie looked at her watch and saw that the time was whizzing by. The woods had been dark to begin with, but now they were darker. *The sun must be setting,* she thought with a shiver.

"Listen," Stephanie said. "It's totally quiet. It's been a long time since I heard another voice." She looked around. "And I'm not even sure which direction we should walk in."

"You might not know, but I do," Mia said.

"Oh, really? Where?"

"There," Mia said. "The path on the right."

Stephanie looked around again. "I don't think so," she said. "I think it's this path. The one to the left."

"No, it's not," Mia insisted.

"Yes, it is!" Stephanie shouted.

"You're wrong!" Mia shot back, pointing to the right. "It's this way."

"No way!" said Stephanie, pointing in the opposite direction. "It's this way!"

CHAPTER 10

◆ ◂ ◆ ◆

For a few seconds Stephanie and Mia stood there, glaring at each other. Finally Mia pulled a penny out of the pocket of her shorts. "We'll flip for it, okay?" she said. "Heads, I win; tails, you lose."

"Very funny," Stephanie said. "Just flip it."

With a snap of her thumb Mia sent the penny spinning into the air. "Call it!" she said.

"Heads!"

The penny landed in the dirt and both girls crouched down to look at it. "It's heads," Stephanie said. "Come on, let's go."

Without a backward glance Stephanie took off

in the direction she'd wanted to go in the first place. In a moment she heard Mia following her, but she didn't slow down. All she wanted to do was find the rest of the class.

As they walked Mia kept muttering about the blisters and the bugs and the boom box. Stephanie bit her lip to keep from shouting at her and walked as fast as she could.

After almost another hour of walking, Stephanie stopped and looked around. "I don't think this is the right way," she said. "We would be back at camp if it was, right?"

"You're asking me?" Mia said. "You're supposed to be the Girl Scout."

Stephanie bit her lip again and didn't say anything. She just kept walking and told herself not to be nervous. Mrs. Walker said all the trails wound up at the campsite. If they just kept following this one, they'd find their way back.

After a few more minutes Stephanie stopped suddenly. All she could see were bushes and ferns and rocks. The path was gone!

Stephanie thought about her father telling her to pay attention while she was hiking. She'd been so mad at Mia, and so anxious to prove she was right about which way to go, that she hadn't even noticed when they'd gone off the path.

"Why'd you stop?" Mia asked, limping up next to her.

Stephanie swallowed hard. "Because we're not on the path anymore," she said.

"Oh, great!" Mia said, looking at the mass of underbrush. "We're lost. That's just great! We're lost in the woods!"

"We're not lost." Stephanie tried to sound confident. She pointed to the right. "Let's try that way." She had no idea if it would lead them back to the campsite, but anything was better than standing around in the darkening woods.

"This can't be the right way," Mia said as they started walking. Then she moaned. "And I think a blister just broke! I knew we should have taken the other path."

Stephanie gritted her teeth. "Look, I won the toss," she said. "So stop complaining, okay?"

"Why shouldn't I complain?" Mia said. "I'm covered with bites and scratches and my feet are a mass of blisters. If we'd gone the way I wanted to go, we'd be back by now."

"If you'd worn the right stuff, you wouldn't have any scratches and blisters," Stephanie said. "If you hadn't brought that stupid, ten-ton boom box along, then we wouldn't have stopped to rest every ten seconds and we wouldn't have lost track of everybody else!"

"Oh, so it's my fault, huh?" Mia said. "Your dad sprayed you with so much insect repellant that the mosquitoes decided to attack me instead and it's my fault?"

"It's your fault as much as mine!"

"Well, excuse me!" Mia said, limping along. She took a deep breath, then said, "What's it like to have such a super-protective dad, anyway?"

Stephanie assumed Mia was making fun of her, and she felt her temperature rise even higher. "Would you stop making remarks about me and my dad? Would you just stop talking so I can listen for the others?"

"Sorreee!" Mia snapped. "I didn't realize you were so bossy."

"And I didn't realize you were more of a troublemaker than everybody says."

"What's that supposed to mean?"

"Never mind," Stephanie said.

"No, I want to know what people say about me," Mia said.

"I'm sure you have a pretty good idea," Stephanie snapped.

"Come on, tell me!" Mia insisted.

"I said forget it!" Stephanie shouted. "Fighting isn't getting us anywhere."

"Well, you're not getting us anywhere either!" Mia shot back. "And it's getting dark, too. What happens when it's totally dark? We'll never find our way back!"

"I have a really strong flashlight," Stephanie said. "We'll be able to see with that." *A flashlight I didn't want to bring,* she remembered. "Now stop griping and start walking!"

"I'm scared," Mia said, sitting down on the ground. "I don't like walking in the dark."

They'd been walking for an hour since they realized they were lost, and it didn't seem like they were any closer to the campsite. It was really dark now, and if it weren't for Stephanie's flashlight, they wouldn't have been able to see anything.

Stephanie sat down next to Mia on top of the

pine needles. "I'm kind of scared too," she admitted. Actually she was starting to feel panicky. "But I really think we should keep walking."

"I can't," Mia said. "There's absolutely no way I'll be able to. I'm too tired and scared."

Stephanie didn't think she'd ever been so frightened in her life. Even though she was pretty sure there weren't any bears in these woods, she didn't like the idea that there were all kinds of other things crawling around in the dark.

"My dad must be worried sick about me," Stephanie said. She could just see him pacing back and forth, wringing his hands, wondering where she was. He'd said to her just the day before that her safety was more important to him than anything. *Poor Dad,* she thought. *I'm sure he's going crazy.*

"It must be nice to have someone worry about you so much," Mia said.

"What do you mean?" Stephanie asked. "Doesn't your mother worry about you?"

"I guess she does in her own way, but she just doesn't ever talk about it," Mia said. "I have a lot of freedom. Mom lets me stay at home by myself all the time."

"Do you have any brothers and sisters?" Stephanie asked.

"No, it's just me and my mom," Mia said. "We've been alone since my dad died."

"My mom died when I was a little girl," Stephanie said.

They looked at each other and shared a sympathetic smile.

"My mom works days and nights, so I don't even see her that much," Mia said. "I don't think she'd know if anything happened to me. I guess it's kind of cool to have the house to myself all the time, but it does get a little lonely once in a while."

Stephanie couldn't imagine being in such an empty house. Her own house was overflowing with people all the time. She didn't think she'd ever been alone in her house in her whole life. Sometimes all the noise and chaos got on her nerves, but she wouldn't trade it for anything.

"I'm sure your mom would be worried about you if she knew you were lost in the woods," Stephanie said.

"I guess you're right," Mia said. "But I think you're really lucky to have a dad who's so protective of you."

"It can be a pain sometimes, believe me," Stephanie said.

"I still think you're lucky," Mia said.

I am lucky, Stephanie realized. Stephanie never had such a strong desire to see her father ever in her life. All she wanted was to run into his big arms and give him a hug.

Stephanie saw two big tears roll down Mia's cheeks. She felt terrible. All that time she thought Mia was just an awful troublemaker, but now she realized how alone she was. She reached into her pack and pulled out Teddy. She'd hidden him there just to be sure nobody found him in her tent.

"Here," she said, holding out the stuffed bear. "Hang on to him for a while. He always makes me feel better when I'm scared and sad."

"That's okay," Mia said, smiling. "I brought my own."

Stephanie watched, amazed, as Mia pulled out her own teddy bear and gave him a big hug.

The girls laughed and hugged their bears, and for a moment they weren't quite as scared.

"I'm hungry," Mia said. "I guess the class is eating s'mores right about now."

"Yeah, you're probably right," Stephanie said sadly.

It was getting even later and the girls were still sitting on the ground holding their teddy bears. They'd decided that the others would definitely come looking for them, and that the best thing to do was to stay in one spot until they were found.

"Speaking of s'mores," Mia started slowly. "I want to tell you I'm sorry about the candy bar thing yesterday."

"I'd rather just forget about it," Stephanie said.

"Well, I can't," Mia said. "I shouldn't have taken them in the first place. They were for everybody to share. At least I haven't eaten any of them. When we get back, I'll give them to Mrs. Jacobs and tell her you didn't have anything to do with it."

"Thanks, Mia," Stephanie said. "Oh, I just remembered! I have some trail mix in my pack." She pulled out the little sack and shared it with Mia.

"What was that?" Mia asked suddenly, pulling her teddy bear closer to her chest.

"What did it sound like?" Stephanie asked, fearing the worst.

"I don't know—it sounded like something moving around in the woods. Maybe I'm just starting to hear things."

"It didn't sound like a bear or anything, did it?" Stephanie felt herself trembling all over.

"I don't know what a bear sounds like," Mia said.

"I don't either," Stephanie said. "And anyway, my dad said there weren't any bears in these woods." *I hope he was right,* she thought, feeling her heart race.

"There, did you hear that?" Mia grabbed Stephanie's hand.

"I definitely heard something," Stephanie said with a gulp. "But I guess there are just a lot of noises in the woods. I mean, the trees probably knock against each other and the birds fly around."

"And the snakes slither on the ground," Mia said.

"Snakes?" Stephanie's jaw dropped open.

"Mrs. Walker was saying last night during her nature talk that there are a lot of snakes in these woods."

"I missed that part," Stephanie said.

Stephanie hated snakes, and she was scared to death that one might crawl on her while she was sitting on the ground. She was miserable. She was trying not to cry. She knew that if she started, the tears would never stop. All she wanted was to be back in her bedroom at home. *I'd even be ecstatic to be playing with Peaches the panda right now,* Stephanie thought longingly.

"Do you want to hear some music?" Mia asked. "I brought some CDs in my pack. At least it would pass the time and it would drown out all these creepy sounds."

Stephanie jumped up excitedly. "Mia! You're a genius!"

"What did I say? I just asked if you wanted to hear some music."

"Exactly! If we play your boom box as loud

as it will go, the others will hear it and they'll come rescue us!"

Mia jumped up too and gave Stephanie a hug. "That's a great idea! My box gets really, really loud."

Mia turned on her boom box and a Pearl Jam song blasted into the woods. She turned the knob to make it as loud as possible, and the two girls were happy for the first time all day.

"I guess we're disturbing the ecosystems," Mia joked.

"Sorry, squirrels!" Stephanie yelled.

"Sorry, bears!" Mia shouted.

"Sorry, raccoons!" Stephanie added.

"Sorry, snakes!" Mia yelled.

"Pearl Jam is my favorite group," Stephanie said.

"Mine, too," Mia said. "Did you see them on that MTV special the other night?"

"No, my dad wouldn't let me stay up that late because I'd been sick." Normally Stephanie would have been embarrassed to admit such a thing, but now she didn't care. "Did your mom let you watch it?"

"Yeah, it was really great," Mia said. "They

did a bunch of songs from the new CD, and Eddie Vedder was cuter than ever." She started tapping her foot to the beat. Stephanie was having a hard time keeping still, too.

"Hey, do you want to dance?" Mia asked.

"Yeah," Stephanie said. "Maybe it will keep the mosquitoes away from you."

Mia laughed and started dancing. Stephanie joined in. And for a moment, neither girl was quite as scared.

CHAPTER 11

"I've never danced in the woods before," Stephanie said breathlessly. For a few moments, Stephanie had almost forgotten that she was lost in the woods. Then she remembered. She tried to push her fears away again, but they kept creeping back.

"You can look at my CDs and see if there's one you like," Mia offered.

Stephanie shone the flashlight into Mia's backpack and pulled out a CD. "Ace of Base!" she exclaimed and popped it in the boom box. "They're one of my favorite groups."

"Here, I'll show you a cool dance to do to

this song," Mia said as she started moving around.

"This is a great dance," Stephanie said. "Where did you learn how to do it?"

"I saw a group do it on MTV late Saturday night," Mia said. "Maybe, if we ever get back to our homes, you could come over and hang out with me some afternoon."

"I'd like that," Stephanie said, trying to keep up with the dance.

"You would?" Mia looked surprised.

"Totally," Stephanie said.

"You don't think they just forgot about us, do you?" Mia asked after a while.

"No way," Stephanie assured her. "I'm positive my dad and everyone else are looking for us. I'm sure someone will be here soon." She was trying to believe her own words, although it was getting harder as the time passed. She was starting to get tired from dancing, but she was afraid to stop. It was the only thing that was calming her nerves.

"I'm having fun dancing and everything," Mia said as a new song started, "but do you think we should be doing something else to try to get rescued?"

"Well, we've done everything we can think of," Stephanie said breathlessly. "We've turned the music up, and the flashlight is shining out into the woods. I can point the light another way so that it can be seen from a different direction," Stephanie said. She put the flashlight on another rock and gazed out into the dark forest. "I don't think we should go any further into the woods," she said. "We'll just get even more lost."

"I guess you're right," Mia said.

Stephanie started dancing again. "Anyway, we can't stop moving," she said. "It's going to keep us from being afraid."

"I'm still afraid," Mia whispered.

"Me, too," Stephanie admitted.

"Stephanie!"

Stephanie turned around and saw her father standing a few feet away. Behind him were Mrs. Walker and three students. The tears that Stephanie had been holding back all night finally let loose.

"Daddy!" she cried. She ran over to her father and jumped up in his arms. She never thought in her whole life that she'd be this happy to see her dad.

"Honey, I was so worried about you," Danny said, wiping a tear off his cheek. "We've been looking for you for hours. The rest of the class is back at the campsite with the other chaperones in case you two had found your way back there."

"I was so scared," Stephanie said, crying in her father's arms. "I didn't know if you'd ever find us."

"We heard the music playing, and we just followed it," Danny said.

Stephanie looked over at Mia, who had turned off the music. She was surrounded by the other students and Mrs. Walker, and she had a big smile on her face.

"Thank goodness for your boom box," Stephanie said to Mia. "It saved our lives."

"It was your idea to play it so loud," Mia said.

"I kept thinking of all the worst things that could have happened to you," Danny said. "And I felt horrible because I know you were mad at me when you left for your hike this morning."

"I've been so silly lately," Stephanie said. "I

was mad about wearing these boots, but they were so much better than sneakers. And I hated it when you sprayed me with repellant, but because you did that, I didn't get one mosquito bite. I didn't want to bring your flashlight along, but thank goodness I did. We would never have gotten through this if we didn't have it."

"You were really brave tonight," Danny said. "This was a terrifying experience you had, but you made the most of it. It was a brilliant idea to play that music. Otherwise, we'd still be looking for you. From now on, I'm going to treat you less like a baby and more like the seventh-grade girl that you are. I guess it's hard for me to accept that you're older now."

"Dad, can you do something for me?" Stephanie whispered in her father's ear.

"Anything," he said.

"Could you give Mia a hug?"

Stephanie followed Danny as he walked over to Mia and gave her a big hug. "I'm so glad you're okay, and I'm so glad you and Stephanie were together," he said to her. "It sounds like you two really helped each other out."

"It was pretty scary," Mia said. "Especially when it got dark."

"We were all really worried about both of you," Danny said.

"That's right," Mrs. Walker said. "I drove to the nearest town and called your mother, Mia, to tell her you were missing, and she broke down on the phone. She's terribly upset."

"Really? She was worried?"

"She was frantic," Mrs. Walker said. "And so was I. As soon as we get back I'll drive you to the phone and you can call her. Now, I think we should all go celebrate and eat some s'mores."

They all started back toward the campsite. Mia stopped for a minute. "Mr. Tanner, Stephanie's lucky to have a dad like you," Mia said.

"And I'm also lucky about something else," Stephanie said.

"What's that?" Mia asked.

"I'm lucky to have a friend like you!"

"You guys must have been scared to death," Allie said to Stephanie.

Everyone was standing around the bus on Monday morning, getting ready to go back home. Stephanie and Mia were being treated like minor celebrities.

"It was pretty creepy," Stephanie said.

"It must have been a drag being stuck with Mia," Hilary said.

"Actually, Mia's great," Stephanie said, looking over at her new friend, who was surrounded by admirers. "She was a good person to be stuck with."

"How did you guys pass the time?" Allie asked.

"We danced," Stephanie said, as if it were the most normal thing to do when lost in the dark woods.

"Allie and I were so scared," Darcy said. "We sat in our tent, crossing our fingers and holding hands, when we heard you were lost."

"It's true," Hilary said. "Both of them were crying."

"I don't know what I would do if anything happened to you," Darcy said.

"Me, either," Allie added.

"There's something I have to tell you," Stephanie said, drawing a deep breath.

"What is it?" Darcy asked. "Something bad?"

"Something dumb," Stephanie said. "I've been feeling jealous of all the time you've been spending with Hilary lately. No offense to you, Hilary, but I was afraid you might replace me as their friend."

"That could never happen in a million years," Allie said.

"I second that," Darcy said.

"The truth is that we've really missed you," Allie said. "First you were gone for so long when you were sick, and then we barely got to see you on this trip."

"I've missed you, too," Stephanie said. "And Hilary, I'd like to spend more time with you. After all, anyone who's friends with my two best friends in the whole world is a friend of mine."

"Okay, class, can I please have everyone's undivided attention?" Mrs. Walker was saying. "I want you to pair up in twos when you get back to school and write a report about your trip. You can write it with whomever you want. I'll leave that up to you."

Stephanie knew exactly who she was going to write her report with. "Hey, Mia, let's write our report together. I think we have a pretty interesting story."

"That's the truth," Mia said. "Why don't you come over after school and we can write it at my house?"

"It's a date!"

The students started getting on the bus, and Stephanie motioned toward Hilary. "Hey, Hilary, come sit with me and Mia on the bus."

"Okay," Hilary said with a smile.

CHAPTER 12

"It sounds like you really had quite an adventure on your camping trip," Joey said. It was Friday night and Stephanie and her family were having dinner in the kitchen. She and her father had just finished telling everyone about the field trip for the fifth time.

"A little more adventure than I expected," Stephanie said.

"I was so proud of Stephanie," Danny said. "When I found her and Mia in the woods, they were dancing around as if nothing was wrong."

"But on the inside, I was scared beyond belief," Stephanie admitted. "We were just dancing to keep ourselves from being too scared."

"I'm getting scared just hearing about what happened to you," Michelle said.

"Me, too," D.J. said.

"That reminds me, there's something I need to thank you for," Stephanie said to Michelle.

"Me?" Michelle pointed to herself.

"Yes, you. I want to thank you for packing Teddy in the bottom of my sleeping bag," Stephanie said. "I don't know what I would have done if he hadn't been with me."

"I have a feeling you would have been just fine without him," Jesse said. "You're really growing up right before our eyes."

"You guys look exhausted," Danny said, looking at Jesse and Becky. "You look like you're the ones who went on a camping trip."

"Well, let's just say that our sweet little twinsters decided that they didn't want to sleep last night," Uncle Jesse said, covering a yawn with his hand.

"I'm still catching up on all the sleep I missed on the camping trip," Stephanie said.

* * *

"Hey, Michelle, how would you like to do something really fun tonight?" Stephanie asked while she was cleaning the dishes with D.J. and Michelle after dinner that night.

"Play stuffed animals?" Michelle asked excitedly.

"Something even more fun that that," Stephanie said, putting a plate in the dishwasher.

"What could be more fun than playing stuffed animals?"

"Camping out," Stephanie said.

"What are you talking about?" D.J. asked. "You just came back from a camping trip. I'd think you'd have had enough wilderness to last you for a while."

"I'm scared to go in the woods after what happened to you," Michelle said.

"We're not going to the woods. I thought we could sleep in our tent in the backyard tonight."

"That sounds super-fun," Michelle said.

"We can bring your stuffed animals in the tent with us," Stephanie said.

"And can we bring special treats to eat?" Michelle asked.

"Great idea," Stephanie said.

"I'll bake some brownies right now for your camping trip," D.J. offered.

"Yippee! I'll go get my animals ready," Michelle said, running out of the kitchen.

"So, was it a total drag having Dad on the trip?" D.J. asked after Michelle had left the room.

"Well, yes and no," Stephanie answered. "It was a pain at first, I must admit. He was giving me so much advice that it really got on my nerves. He even tied the laces on my boots in front of the whole class."

"That sounds like Dad," D.J. said, smiling.

"When our class went swimming, he made me wear a life jacket," Stephanie said.

"When I went on my sixth-grade camping trip, he told the teacher that I had to go in a canoe with an adult," D.J. said. "I was totally humiliated. When I got back, I wouldn't talk to him for a week."

"I was pretty mad, too," Stephanie said. "But I finally realize that what you said was true."

"Which words of older-sister wisdom are you referring to?" D.J. asked.

"What you said about not being able to change Dad," Stephanie explained. "Not only did I figure out that there's no use trying to change him, I realized something else."

"You did?"

"Yeah," Stephanie said. "I realized that sometimes he's actually right, and I should listen to what he says."

"What was that?" Michelle asked, sitting up in the tent. "I think I heard a bear or a lion or something."

Stephanie couldn't help smiling. "There aren't any bears or lions in our backyard, Michelle. That was just Nicky or Alex crying about something."

"Are you sure?"

"Positive. The only bear in this backyard is right here." Stephanie held up Teddy.

"Aren't you scared?" Michelle asked, sliding her sleeping bag closer to Stephanie's.

"I'm not scared because there's nothing to be afraid of here," Stephanie said. "But it's okay if you *are* scared. I was scared in the woods when I got lost with Mia."

"Did you cry?"

"I didn't cry until Dad came and found us," Stephanie said.

"You're really brave," Michelle said. "I would have cried the whole time if I was lost in the woods."

"I have an idea. Let's sing a song so you won't be scared."

"Can we sing 'If I Could Talk to the Animals,' from *Dr. Doolittle?"*

"I love that song," Stephanie said, starting to sing.

Halfway through the song Danny stuck his head in the tent. "Hey, girls, I see you're still awake," he said.

"We were just a little scared, so we thought singing would make us feel better," Michelle said.

"Steph, there's something I need to talk to you about," Danny said in a serious voice.

Oh, no, Stephanie thought. *He's going to tell me that after all the excitement, I need my rest or I'll have a relapse!* "What is it?" she asked.

"I wanted to tell you that I've been thinking a lot about what happened on the camping trip, and I've come to a decision," Danny said.

"What's that?" Stephanie asked.

"I've decided to try not to be so protective of you," Danny said. "You've shown me that you can really take care of yourself. I know I can be too smothering sometimes."

"That's okay. I realize now that I'm lucky to have a father like you who cares so much about me."

"I guess we both learned a lot this weekend," Danny said, kissing Stephanie on the forehead.

"Look, it's Comet!" Michelle squealed as the dog ran into their tent. "I guess he wants to camp out, too."

"Well, there's enough room for him in our tent, I guess," Stephanie said. "What do you think, Michelle, should we let him camp out with us?"

"Yes! He'll protect us from the bears and lions!"

Suddenly a platter of brownies appeared inside the tent flap. Michelle's eyes grew big.

"I finally finished making the brownies," D.J. said, crawling in and putting the plate down in the center of the tent.

"They look delicious!" Michelle said.

"Thanks, Deej." Stephanie grabbed a brownie.

"I think I'll have one of those," Danny said, popping one in his mouth.

"Am I hearing things?" D.J. asked. "It sounds like Nicky or Alex is crying in the backyard."

Jesse poked his head into the tent, carrying Nicky, who was crying hysterically in his arms. "Hey, guys, did Comet carry Nicky's blanket in here?"

"I don't see it," Stephanie said.

"He won't be able to go to sleep without his blanket," Jesse said.

"Here, Nicky, have a brownie," D.J. said.

Everyone watched as Nicky studied the brownie in his hands, then put it in his mouth. Suddenly the crying stopped, and everyone clapped.

"Those must be magical brownies," Michelle said. "Maybe I should have another one."

"I was just reading a book in my room when I smelled the distinct odor of brownies wafting through the window," Joey said, crawling into the tent. "I followed my nose, which never fails me."

"Would you like a brownie?" D.J. said.

"Oh, hey, thanks," Joey said, grabbing two of them.

Just then Becky poked her head into the tent. "There you are!" she said to Jesse. She was carrying Alex, who was crying. "I looked all over the house for you."

"What's Alex so upset about?" Jesse asked.

"I think he missed Nicky," Becky said. "Can I have a brownie?"

"Give one to Alex," Michelle suggested. "It'll make him feel better."

"This is kind of cozy with everyone in the tent like this," Joey said with a big yawn.

"Look, Nicky fell asleep in Uncle Jesse's arms," Stephanie whispered.

"Great. I'm afraid I'll be stuck here all night," Jesse said. "If I stand, he'll wake up screaming."

"If I take Alex away from Nicky, he'll go ballistic again," Becky said. "I guess I'm stuck here, too."

"Guess who else is here for the night?" Stephanie said. She pointed to Joey, who was sound asleep and snoring loudly.

"Well, if everyone else is sleeping here, I guess I will, too," D.J. said.

"How about you, Dad?" Stephanie asked. "I think you should stay in the tent with us."

"Are you sure you want me on this camping trip?" Danny asked.

Stephanie laughed. "It wouldn't be the same without you, Dad. Just don't try to tie my shoes in the morning."